Squirmy Wormy

Words by Rosa Clark

Pictures by RJ Glosser

DEDICATION

For Easton – Sorry it took me so long to publish *your* book. Love you, little dude.

ACKNOWLEDGEMENTS

Thank you to my son for his patience with publishing this book. Thank you to my dad for illustrating it way before I was on a self-publishing journey. Thank you to the readers, big and small for taking the time to build vocabulary with my youngest readers. Rhyming is an essential part of learning to read.

Squirmy Wormy is a squeaker.

Squirmy Wormy wears a sneaker.

Squirmy Wormy learns to shoot.

Squirmy Wormy
wears a boot.

Squirmy Wormy is a flipper.

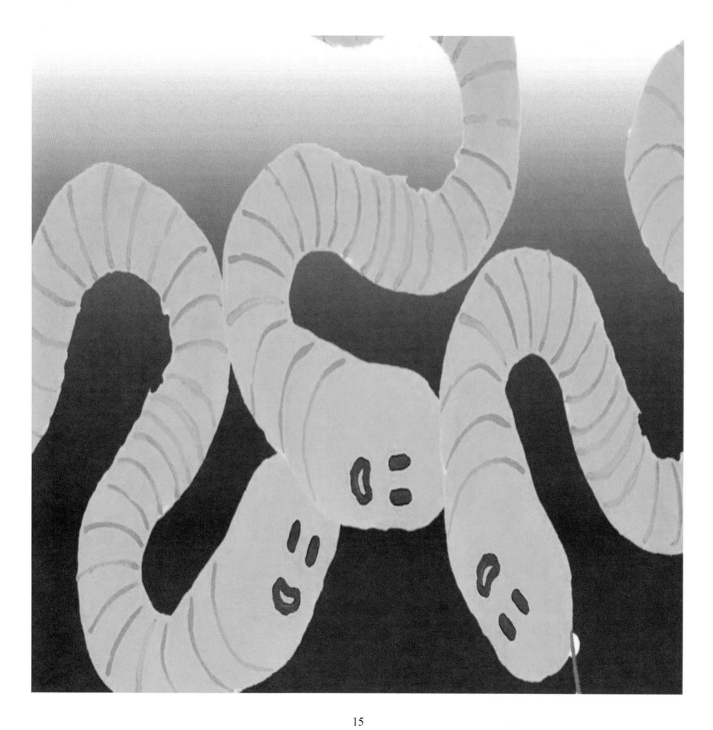

Squirmy Wormy
wears a slipper.

Squirmy Wormy blows out a candle.

19

Squirmy Wormy
wears a sandal.

Squirmy Wormy
wears a shoe.

Squirmy Wormy says, "I love you."

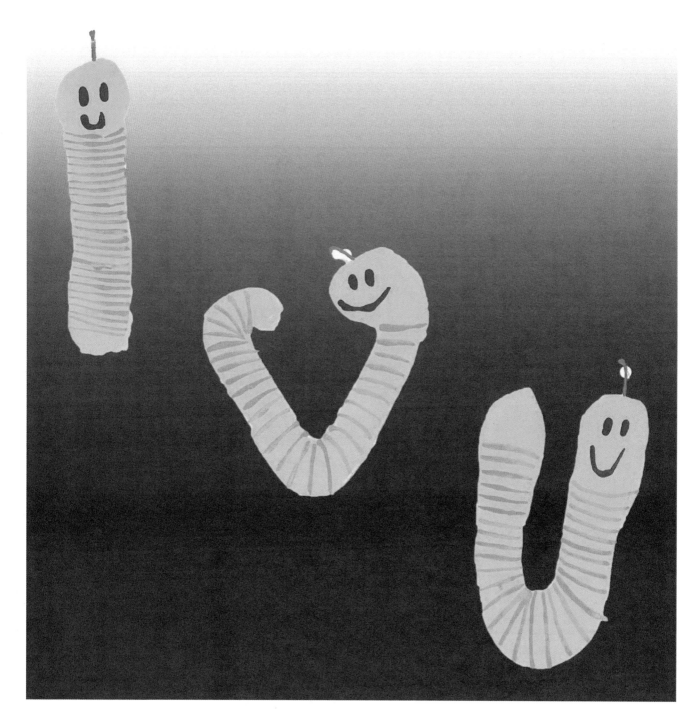

ABOUT THE AUTHOR

Rosa Clark is the mom of two wonderful children. She is also the author of Princess Zoom Zoom Loses Her Zoom, Squirmy Wormy, and Wiggle Piggle.

Made in the USA
Monee, IL
22 December 2022